Pretty
from the back

Pretty
from the back

SHARON A. WHITE

authorHOUSE®

AuthorHouse™ LLC
1663 Liberty Drive
Bloomington, IN 47403
www.authorhouse.com
Phone: 1-800-839-8640

Published by AuthorHouse   11/23/2013

ISBN: 978-1-4918-1302-7 (sc)
ISBN: 978-1-4918-1301-0 (hc)
ISBN: 978-1-4918-1300-3 (e)

Library of Congress Control Number: 2013916115

CONTENTS

For Mom and all the Women in my Family
and my granddaughter Kaliyah

Special thanks to my Family and Sister friends for your encouragement

Sheila L.White, Lorell Pitts Johnson, Victoria White Chears,
Gavin L. Burr, Sharon Christmas, Reginald White, Richard White,
Ronald White, Roderick White, Pauline Ford Springfield,
Kevin Taylor, Sandra Wetzman

Special thanks to Kayla

WHITE FOOTPRINTS

I see white footprints in my dreams
I see footprints in my dreams!
They're WERE BIG white footprints
Should I be scared?
Or should I say
Thank you,
Thank you . . .
Thank you . . .

BIG FOOTPRINTS

I saw white footprints in my dream
I felt a lightness of heart
I felt the warmth of his arms carrying me
                                          From within
They were big footprints

Shades of grey illuminant . . . . my dream

I felt silence like I never felt before
                                          From within

I saw white footprints in my dream
They were big footprints

I felt at peace,
I felt at peace

I felt whole
I felt loved

I feel GOD

I saw white footprints in my dream!

And now I see this Golden Glow

My bone says
THANK YOU,

IT'S MY HEART

It's the wanting that hurts the most
It's the silence that makes the wound bleed
It's not your touch that burns

It's the wanting

It's the love that you marinade into my soul
It's the love I want to marinade back to yours
It's not your touch that burns

It's the wanting

It's my heart . . . . that yearns the loudest

It's the wanting
It's the wanting

DEFINITION OF VICKIE

Life's circle of sadness
Has wrapped itself
Around my heart
I must admit
I have no more
Room
For
B.S.

CACTUS V.P.

MY BOY

Another Mother heart has broken
Knowing she has lost
He has attacked her heart for years
Practice, Practice
Another black son has lost his way
Lost his soul
Lost his mind
A mislaid future
She misses the boy, he was
And hides from the man he is

Her guilt, his journey
His secrets, her love
Her denial, his shame
His pressure,her spirit
Her blame, her pain
His fear, his love
His nerve, her critic's

She never shared her guilt
He never shared his journey
She never believed he was and is the guiltiest
They shared the blame
And now she watches

He has his own cage
He has his own pain
He has his own guilt
They never shared the
LOVE

ECHOES OF ROMANCE

Whispers of romance echoes in the breeze
Do you remember me?
I remember you
Catching a foul ball is easier
Than believing in the "Great White Hope of Love"
Or love at first sight
First kiss
I like spin the bottle
You make me weak in the knees
Whispers of sadness echoes in the breeze
I remember you
Do you remember me?
I remember heart to hearts
I remember regrets
I remember sad good-byes
I remember echoes of romance
I remember whisper of love
I remember
I remember you
Do you?
Remember Me?

FIVE DOLLAR MAN

I know this man
They call him five dollar man
He has a story and a smile just for you
Don't look him in the eyes, his sadness draws in your love
He is a man of all season
In the winter time, he says, let me have five dollars
In the springtime, he says, let me have ten dollars
In the summertime, he says, let me have five
Let me have
Let me have
Let me have
Mr. Five Dollar Man
Never says thank you
His eyes gazes over yours
Not all fantasy makes the front page
Mr. Five Dollar Man
Has a new title
He has graduated with honors
We now call him
Twenty Dollar Man
My Brother, My Brother, My Brother

"HOW LONG"

How long can you hold on to the fairy tale of love?
As long as you want to
How long do you hold onto a memory of a kiss?
Until the sensation disappears from your lips
How long do you hold onto the pain of love?
As long as you forget, what love is all about
How long does it take to forgive?
Forever or a day
Forever or a day
How long does it takes to tell someone you love them?
As long as time gives you
How long does it take to stop wanting him?
As long as your heart say so"
How long can this dream go on?
Until the sandman says no more
How long?
How Long?
How long does it takes to let go?
As long as I say, so"

TO MOM

My Sister' a
Why you hurt me
My Sister Friend
Why you call me Bitch
My Sister Girl
Why do you talk about me that way
My Sister, My Sister
Why don't you love yourself
My Sister' a
Why can't you see Yourself
My Sister, My Sister
Why you put me Down like that
My Sister Friend
Why can't you Respect me and you
My Sister, My Sister
Why do you have so much Pain
My Sister Friend
Why don't you open your Heart to Love yourself First
My Sister Girl
Why can't you Forgive
Do you know the Word Worthy
My Sister Friend
Do you know the words "It takes a Sisterhood to Raise a Real Sister A"
My Sister Girl, My Sister Friend, My Sister My Sister
I Do Honor You

SARAH'S UNICORN

Whenever I see Sarah's
Unicorns come to play
I Wonder
Butterflies fill her Crown
Men Fantasize about Women like Sarah
Unicorns and Sarah have the same Aura
Mythical
Mysterious
Magic
I see Sarah Dancing with Unicorns in the wild Rose of Sharon
Weeping Cherry tress enjoy the view
Sarah style Hair of Lily's
Eye's that Shine,
Leg's that never end
Things are not always what they Seem in Sarah's World

"That Pigeon Toe Girl"

Sometimes letting go takes Years

Even Open Wounds, take time to Heal

I loved to Men Once
One made me Smile Big
The Other made me Smile even Bigger
I met One on a Cool Summer Night
The Other One I met on a Rainy fall Night,
Every Girl should have one flat tire and one leading Man
Romance
Lost Love
Give Me Love
One was Tall
The Other was even Taller
Give Me Love
Lost Love
One made me Feel Loved all the way Down to my Pearly Toes
The Other One Touched my Heart
One told me his Mother called me, that nice Girl from Gary'
The Other One Grandmother said,' you like that Pigeon Toe's
Girl'
Give Me Love
Lost Love
One made me Want to see the World
The Other One Gave me Flowers
I Married the One who Asked Me
One called to ask would I ever Forgive Him
The Other One called to say, you were Always the One
Give Me Love
Lost Love

I Loved Two Men Once
And they both Made the Same Mistake
They Loved Themselves More
Give Me Love
Lost Love

"ALL ABOUT ME"

Something Touch Me
In the Blackness of the Night
Something touch me
I wasn't Dreaming
I wasn't sucking my Thumb
I wasn't Dreaming
I wasn't Dreaming of Lose
I wasn't Dreaming of Love
I wasn't Dreaming at all
Something woke me in the Night
It was loneliness
And Someone was Sucking my Thumb
Me

"MY GOLDEN DREAM"

I often Dreamed I lived on Old Oak Tree House
In the mist of the Stars
I dance the Naked dance of Love
And the Moon Shines on.

How unreal, it seem to others
But it was real for me
Dream a little, Dream with me
Dreams do come true.

I always looked at Trees as a Gift from Mother Earth
Enormous Gift that never goes away
Dream a little, Dream with me.

In the Morning drew of my Golden Dream
Norah Jones sits gracefully on an Old Elm Tree Branch
Singing "Come Away With Me"
I looked to see Tree Branches swaying to the song
Dream a little ,Dream with me.

I see the Pink Weeping Cherry Tree
Changing colors with the Rhythm of the song
Pink to White
To Red with Love
Dream a little, Dream with Me

Around Midnight Blue
Chris Botti comes out with his Magic Horn to Play "Light the Stars"
Even the Sour Wood Trees gives him the Nod.
Dream a little, Dream with Me

All this Happens in my Tree House of Dreams
Dream a little, Dream with Me

Sometimes Dreams Do Come True.

"Taste of Honey"

Don't lick my Tattoo
Your Lips will taste like Honey
You will like it.

Don't Smell my Skin
It's too Aromatic you will lose yourself in Me.
You will like it.

Don't ask me for my Sweet Spot
You should Enjoy the Journey
You will like it.

Don't Love me too Much
You should Desire me More
Then I will Love you Back
You will love it.

USED TO

I used to Dream about you
I talk in my Sleep
I thought you were Real
I remember your Smile
I used to Dream about you

Now I Just Wish Upon a Star
I just Won the Lottery
I remember your Glow
I used to Dream about you
    I Blush in my Dreams
I remember my Glow with you
I used to Dream about you
Now I just Sleep

HOPE, GRATITUDE, LOVE

I Woke with the Sun Shinning
Purple Glow on my Toes
With Hope and need , fighting to be First
I Woke with a Heavy Heart
Gratitude is Shouting
Me, Me, Me,
Love is asking
What about me, What about me
And the Sun is Still Shinning

NEVER UNDERSTOOD

I never understood love
Is it moonbeam's that signal your heart to Love?
Or do you glow in the dark, whenever you think of him
How does Love work.

I Chased a Man once
Around a Tree
Down the Street
On a Bus
To a Party
Took his Jacket just to catch his eye

It was Love at First Sight
Give that girl a Apple
Is that Love?

Or are you just a Libra holding the Scale
How does Love work?
Do Particles Flow Skin to Skin
And Guide you to each Other
Is that how Love works

Or do Body parts catch on Fire
At eye Contact
Is that Love

I never understood Love
I've been walking around in circles all my Life
Looking for Love
I just haven't been loved right.

"END IN TEARS"

My Tears come easy on Rainy Days
*　　　　Raindrops of Love come First*
Tears of Lost come Second
*　　　　Raindrops of Hope come Third*

Tears for forgotten memories come Last
*　　　　Clusters of Tears, Cloud my Eyes*
Sweet Nectar of Mother"s Love
loves me back

It always began with a Smile and end in Tears

Rainy Days
Rainy Days
Rainy Days

"HATE"

I woke up this Morning thinking of things
I hate more than you

Bad Mouth
Not True
I hate you More
Bad Children
Not True
I hate you even More

Nasty People
Not True
I do hate you More

Bad Drivers
Not True
I really do hate you More

Snow in Winter
Not True
I really, really, do hate you More

My High School Gym Teacher
Not True
I'm sure I hate you More

I hate Rats
Not True
That's an Equal hate

What I can't believe
What I haven't said
What everyone, else sees
What took me so long
What I Hate More
Is being
Married To You!!!!!!!!

"SIBLING"

I often wonder why sibling can't
Be like rain drops, Something Fresh.
I often wonder why sibling can't
Be like the pet you loved.
I often wonder why sibling can't
Be like a breeze on a hot day.
I often wonder why sibling can't
Be like a cold drink of water, something to look
forward to.
I often wonder was I
The
Milk Man Baby

"BEST LOVE"

Love hasn't touched my Lips
The Warmth of the sun Heats my Heart
I do feel
The wind kiss my Cheeks
I Blush
I came from places of Love
Lonely Love
Romantic Love
Minnie Riperton Love
Tender Love
Monkey Love
Deceitful Love
Friend Love
Silly Love
Free Love
Secret Love
Puppy Love
Runaway Love
Worthless Love
Intense Love
Sweet Potato Love
Lost Love
Foolish Love
Patience Love
Sad Love
Good Love
The Best Love of all

God Loves Me

"I Wanted To Be"

Never wanted to be a Girl Scout
I wanted to be a Cub Scout,
I would have looked good in that Blue Uniform
I wanted to be a Wolf Scout
I wanted to be a Eagle Scout
I w   anted to be a Boy
Dad said No!!!!!!
I never wanted to be a Girl Scout
Who wants to be a Brownie.

"SORBET"

He likes when i bake Cookies
I like Raspberry Sorbet.
He likes to talk late into the night
something about the Stars
I like the Sound of his Voice.

He likes the way i Breath
I like his Gentle Touch
He likes Kissing Me
I think his Kisses are Dry.

He likes my Cookies
I like Lemon Sorbet
He likes it when i call him "Pappi Chulo"
I think about not calling him anything

He likes his Big Ego
I think his Ego is getting in the way
He Likes Me
I like him Sometimes
But Not Today

%%%%%%

I don't like XMAS
       Santa forgot my address long time ago
I don't like the Easter Bunny
       Boil eggs make me sick
I don't like Barbie Dolls
       My Mom said that's not the image i wanted for you
I don't like Mondays
       I just need one more day to Sleep
I don't like Rain Storms, Hurricanes, Hail, or Thunderstorms
and one more
I don't like
The other 53%%%%%

"ON THE EDGE"

In the pity of my darkness
on the edge of my sin
loneliness, comforts
My Black Heart

Leave me to my darkness
there are no illusions
of self
no father to love

on the edge of my sinful life
naked strangers
dance into darkness
there's no secrets

in the middle of my pity
in the middle of my madness
darkness sings

Welcome Home
Your Pit is Ready

INVISIBLE WOUNDED

I like being invisible
You can't see my hollow heart of hurt!!
Just call me Vessel
Only the wounded can see me.

I like the clear Space of me
It's hard to be Bitter
When the Structure of me is
less than Tissue
Just call me Vessel.

I like being light Heartened
It only means
I'm Divorce from my
Emotional need of you.

I like being invisible
Only the Wounded can see me
Hear Me,
Feel Me,
Love Me, Back

TIC-TAC-TOE

I thought i was Dreaming or was I
Phone Ringing
Someone was Kissing, me Softly down my back
It stopped in the middle and played
Tic-Tac-Toe with his Tongue
I was laughing in my sleep
I thought i was alone
I felt him
Dark room
Hot Bed
Someone, but No one

But than he said
What about Me!!!!!

MY SOUL TO KEEP

I wander around the world Etching
    Thin lines of your name into clouds
Challenging my heart to forgive, to forget, to exhale
    My soul sings to anyone who listens

I wander around the world in Gloom
    Darkness calls me his lover

Etching of thin lines keeps the clouds at bay

I wander around the world

Challenging my heart to open
Challenging my heart to let visitors in
Challenging my heart to pray and wait
Challenging my Soul to come Home

TO MY LITTLE FRIEND J

Good morning world J shouts out the car window
his smile says look at me I'm happy
i turned to see joy running from his face
Good morning world he shouts again
i asked why are you so happy
can't you see the birds flying around
can't you smell the trees
and look at that blues sky
i think this little boy has been here before
this time we both shout out the window
"Good Morning World"

SHARON 1, 2, 3

I had two amazing friends name Sharon 1,2,
Sharon K. was small in stature but was Bold, Exciting, and a little
bit Brazen, Vulnerable, and Sensitive. she was all that I wanted to be.
She had smooth chocolate skin, her smile was like cotton candy.

Her laugh began with a chuckle, turn into a rumble, ended in a roar.
We laughed, we cried, we had babies, and laughed some more. She had
that extra something she had Dimples.!!
I miss my friend
I miss my Juicy Fruit.!!!

Sharon A. She is what you call Statuesque.
I always envied those long legs, those long eyelashes.
She has a confidence in her walk, she makes me smile with each stride,
she carries her head high. I'm woman hear me roar. She is Bold. Exciting,
Volatile, Sensitive, Vulnerable, Ambitious. and Religious, but most
importantly she is a Survivor. I colored my hair Fiery Engine Red once,
she colored her hair Fiery Engine Red also, she was one hot mama. After
all these years we still call it the Red Summer. We laughed, we cried, we
had babies and laughed some more. She has that something extra, she
showed me the true meaning of friendship, in my darkest days when I
thought no light at the end of my tunnel. Sharon A. would say GOD
loves you, I love you, your baby boy loves you, baby girl this will be OK.

Even now when I have my dark moments, I hear her voice saying,
baby girl this will be OK GOD loves you.

MY GRAND LUCILLE

I smell the Mississippi River calling me home
She made homemade biscuits from scratch
When Sonny Boy came home
That's the way she said, I loved you to him
My Grand Lucille Thomas Dewberry

Peach tree in the backyard makes the house smell "Heavenly"
Yellow Apron with Flowers
Bow Legs
Busch Beer
Black Skin
Raleigh cigarettes on the Kitchen table
Banana Pudding in the icebox
My Lucille
Childhood memories of love
"Ray Charles" playing in the background "Hit the Road Jack"
Hillary Dewberry out hunting, for rabbit, squirrels, and deer
5915 Ridges Street, "Saint Louis Missouri"
B.B. King have his Lucille
But I had the Original
My Grand Lucille Thomas Dewberry
I Miss Her
I miss her homemade biscuits
I Miss that taste of love

IN THE RAIN

Eye's closed
thunder roars
Joyless memories rumbling from within
a nude woman in the night, plays a violin in the rain
all in the streets of my mind
Who are you?
rain Dreams
Dream rain
I do like the thunder
sleep come
Dream ends
I smile when i dream

IN MY REALITY

Loneliness holds me close
I hold myself just to feel

    My sadness has a voice of it's own
    In fact i thought it was Morgan Freeman
    Talking to me like an old friend

In reality Morgan Freeman was on T.V.
Playing God.

Loneliness Wins Again.

MY LIFE

I live my life though someone else window
I live my life though someone else plan
Peek a Boo
Crack your window
I can't see me
Do you see me
I used to be a distance runner
run, baby, run,

I live my life cold

HIDE YOUR CHEEKS

After i said i loved you
I felt a warm breeze kiss my check
Flashes of light, hide behind my eye's
And you vanished
What do you see?
After that
The kiss on the cheek sting like a
Bee

Freaking Kidding me, Right

Stillness of grey has made it presents known
Silver Bells, silver bells
I kind of like it
Do it have to be so White?
Wearing black and White looks good on me
Do placement of grey hair really matters, to whom
Do i have to agree with all the placements, I think not
How often can one grey hair grow under your chin, out of your ear, on
your eyelid, in your nose, on your eyebrow, under your arm on your chest,
on your toes, on your face, who knew?
How about that one place, you know that one place when you
Discover that first grey hair,
You just have to say.

"You have to be freaking Kidding Me," You have to be Freaking Kidding Me.
This could make you cry, and laugh at the sometime.
No one talks about that!!

They talk about your bones, so what
They talk about your white tooth, so what
They talk about dryness, OK, OK
They talk about that little blue pill. really, so what

But never about the beauty of the grey
Some how they want you to believe that
Grey and sadness go together and not
Grey and Wisdom
Grey and Desire
Grey and Compassion
Silver Belles
Silver Bells
Silver Bells

LOVE BORROWED

I'm a borrower
I borrowed love from Mom
to give to Dad
They didn't know how to love each other

I borrowed love from Sheila Lynn
to give to Debra Ann
she needed more love than me

I borrowed love from Dad
To give to Vickie Pearl
She needed to know we all loved her
I'm the original borrower

I borrowed love from Aunt Polly
to give to K. T.
I didn't want him to me lonely

So now my love is low
I wonder, who will borrow
Love for me.

GOD NOT MAN

I believe in God
I believe in Jesus Christ
I believe in love at first sight
I believe if you have inner Peace you have everything
I believe in driving a Sport Car once in your life, Red
I believe in Meditation
I believe in eating a Good Hamburger
I believe in honoring your Mother and Father even when they make it hard.
I believe their is Spirits among us
I believe James Baldwin was one of the best American Writers
I believe in Prayer
I believe if you call him Jehovah he will answer
Others call him our Father, he will answer
Others call Savior he will answer
Do you believe
I believe
I believe in all faiths
Baptists
Pentecostal
Judaism
Hinduism
Buddhism
Lutheran
Methodist
Protestant
Orthodox
Episcopal
The real question is not what religion to believe
The real question is not how faithful you are
The real question is how do you believe in Man

RAINY DAYS VOW

My wedding vow
For a rainy day
I asked God to show me how to love
He sent me you
I asked God for this day
We said I do
I asked God for family and friends to share our love
He sent them
I asked God
To live with me
He said I Do

Sweet Monkey Love

Do you know anything about Monkey love?
Have you ever felt Monkey love?
Let me tell you about Monkey love

Monkey love makes your heart smile
That's what you call romantic Monkey love.

Monkey love wakes you up blushing
that's what you call color me red
Monkey love

Monkey love,
Give me that sweet, Monkey Love

Monkey love gives you that Joker smile
you know the guy from batman smile baby smile
Monkey love,
Give me that sweet Monkey love

I have that Octopus Monkey Love
I need all eight arms to keep
You close to my heart,
My lips
My neck
My arms
My Joy

Monkey Love, Monkey Love
give me that sweet Monkey Love

I WANT IT BACK

I've seem to forgotten how to smile
Smiling seem to be a, lost art among black woman
Have all black woman forgotten how to smile or is it just me?
Have all that tight weave taken our smile?
Have all those long extensions taken our joy?
I used to have that tickle me smile, I want it back
I used to smile just because it felt good
Someone or something has taken my smile and i want it back
I want it back
How long can you hide from your smile
About as long as you can lie to yourself about a man
Forever or a Day
forever or a Day
I want it back
I want my tickle me smile back
To all
To all
I will give you one Wig
For one week of Sunshine Smiles
I will give you all the extensions you want
For two weeks of Happy Smiles
I will give you a Whole Weave
for one month of God give me this Smile
I just want our smiles back
I want my tickle me smile back
I want it back
I want it back
tickle me

TREE LOVE

Tree of time echo in the breezes
I know you love me
Sweet grass
Sweet dreams
In the Land of Sweet Honey, Unicorns, come to play
Tree of time blooms into love
Take my Tenderness away
Leave me my blues
I walked to, the top of the tree
Only to smile at the sky
You do love me . . . ?

CHOCOLATE GIRL

This Girl has a sweet chocolate glow about her
But her eye's never meet yours
She has that look and sadness is not even the right word
Her eyes has dullest of color
Her smile is small
This sweet chocolate girl has encounter life
Her only possession is her pain

I cry inside for her
I see her unable to speak
I see the pain in her eyes
I weep openly
She still has that look
Tears never come

What's hidden behind her eyes { rage }
Her smile is a surprise
She has small steps
You can't hear her
I love this sweet chocolate girl

Sleeps with her hands over her ears
Her movements are control my fear

What happen to this sweet chocolate girl?
She still has that chocolate glow

"Do You Know"

To my girlfriends who I love and respect as my sisters.
Do you have to carry!!
Do you have to carry the pain with so much pride?
Do you know how hard it is?
Do you know how hard it is to watch?
Your Mother, your Sister, your Daughters, your Friends,
Do you know!!
To carry that much pain around your heart.
Around your head
In your face
in your soul
Do you know?
So many of us just do
Some just wear the pain for armor
Some just make friends with unhappiness
We should ask the pain
Will you still love me tomorrow?
Shame on you for smiling at your pain
Shame on you for making friends with unhappiness
Sometime you have to sugar coat madness and love
Yourself first
Some time you have to sugar cost madness
and let God be your armor, your friend, your pain, your joy

Your Madness!!!!!!

UNDER MY BREATH

Four year old little boy name Hilton urinate on my bathroom floor.
I asked him why?

He replied the sun is a star, not a planet
I called him baby
He replied, 'I'm not a baby, I'm upset with you for calling me baby'

Under my breath
I called him smelly cat, smelly cat, what have you ate today.

Four year old little girl name Sabrina fingertips touched my skin, she
said.
You have brown skin something must be wrong with you.
I asked her why
she replied with a smile
I replied you have red hair something must be wrong with you
She replied yes
under my breath i said smelly cat, smelly cat what have you ate
today.

My Mother said to me one day, you look better from the back then
you do from the front
I pause
I replied with a smile and walked away
under my breath i said smelly cat, smelly cat what have
you ate today?

HONEY POT

I Woke up today smiling to myself
I remember
I remember something that i Forgotten
Love, Love
I forget that Love makes you Warm
I forget that Love makes you Happy
I had a feast today
It felt good to remember Love
Not Romantic Love
Just Love
Not Ancient Love
Just Love
Not Woo Woo love
Just Love
I remember Love today
Maybe tomorrow
I'll remember
What my Honey Pot is for,

Love

My life as a Smelly Cat

*Tim thinks he cries because i said naught' things to him , My favorite
naught words to him is No!
under my breath i say
smelly cat, smelly cat what have you ate today,
then i said!!! Why Me*

*Kayla thinks he cries because, he doesn't get to eat snacks all day long the
way he wants.
My favorite words are
eat a apple!
Under my breath i say
smelly cat, smelly cat, what have you ate today
then i said!!! Why, Why, Why*

*Jack thinks he, cries because, I put him in time out, I think he thinks if
he screams really loud you will give him his way.
My favorite words to him! Go for it
I know how to scream too. do you want to have contest?
under my breath i say
smelly cat, smelly cat, what have you ate today
then i said!!! Only You*

*Joe thinks he cries because, I sent him to his room.
yes, yes, yes, yes, yes, yes, yes
I gave myself time out
My favorite words for him
it's not always about you
under my breath i say
smelly cat, smelly cat, what have you ate today
then i said!!!! Really, Really, Really*

*Ana thinks he cries because, he wants to go outside, i think he likes
making crying faces*

My favorite words for him
Acting school, real tears are wet
under my breath i say
smelly cat, smelly cat, what have you ate today
then i said!!! Why me, Why Me

Jim thinks he cries, and cries because, he thinks, he should have his way
all the time. I think he is right, but he just can't have his way with me all
the time.
My favorite words for Jim
crying is good for you try smiling and crying at the same time
under my breath i say
smelly cat, smelly cat what have you ate today
then i said!!!! Only You, Only You

Joshua thinks he cries because, he only wants to eat carrots, i think he
cries for attention, he has this mischievous smile on his face
My favorite words for Joshua
You look pretty when you cry, go for it
Under my breath i say
smelly cat, smelly cat, what have you ate today
then i said!!!!! Really, Really

Tom thinks he cries because, he says naughty words, i think he
likes saying naughty words, and I tell him "shut it down"
My favorite words for Tom
I will do soap, water, in mouth
Under my breath i say
smelly cat, smelly cat, what have you ate today
then i said!!! You would Think

Ava thinks she cries because she doesn't like listening, she likes to me right all the
Time, I think she has a hard time with the words, No, Stop, Not Right Now
My favorite words to him
It's not just about you
under my breath i say

smelly cat, smelly cat, what have you ate today
then i said!!! Only you, just one night

John thinks he cries because ,he knows ,I know he's playing the big baby.
big baby. big baby
my favorite words for John
Baby's do grow up, grow baby, grow
under my breath i say
smelly cat. smelly cat what have you ate today
then i said!!!! Why Me

Gavin thinks he cries because, he wants to go to the park. I think he
likes to cry, when you don't do what he says
My favorite words for Gavin
You do know, you are not the Boss, of me
under my breath i say
smelly cat, smelly cat, what have you ate today
then i said, if Only

I cry because I have to listen to Joe, Joshua, Jack, John, Tim, Tom, Ava
Ana, Kayla, Gavin

Smelly Cat, Smelly Cat
What have you ate today!!!

TALKING TENNIS

After talking to you
I always walk away thinking.
What just happen
Who said what?
I started this
Why?

You talk too fast
I talk too loud
Was i laughing too much
Was i the talking too much
I do know one thing

Talking to you reminds me of watching tennis at Wimbledon
Big., Big, question
Who was the Server?
Who was the Receiver?
Who had match point?
Who has Love???

BEAUTIFUL SMILE

E-mailed this line to three friends.

I woke up this morning thinking about a "Tall Dark Fat Man but He
Had your Beautiful Smile"

My brother Richard was the first to call back. Who are you calling
fat, and dark can i call you tall
He only said no, not this brother,
before he hung up
I whisper you do have a Beautiful Smile

E-mailed are a good way to start your day!!!

The next call came from old forgotten friend
So you were thinking about me, He said
I said are you a "Tall Dark Fat Man With A Beautiful Smile"
He said no I'm a short around fat man,
I'm Pumpkin Eater
before he hung up
I whisper you do have a Beautiful Smile.

Third call, from my Mother
she said are you still daydreaming about a "Tall Dark, Fat Man with
a Beautiful Smile
I said Yes
She said
Why daydream
find that tall dark rich fat man with that beautiful smile
Why don't live your life?
I said
Yes, but can i still dream

SHADOW MAN

I see a shadow of a man, on the wall
He stands in my kitchen
He watches me cook
He watches me clean
He just watches me
I should be scared
I should be scared
Not scared
I know him

I see a shadow of a man, down the hall
He watches me
He on the side of me
He walks with me
I should be scared
I should be scared
Not scared
I know him

There's a spirit in my bedroom
It watches me sleep
It touches my toes
I feel something
I'm Scared
Hi Daddy

Sweet Marmalade

Forgotten pain
Never leaves you
It hangs under your breath
Tell no secret
Tell no lies
A grazed over life
Insanity looks goods

Taste of Sweet Marmalade covers the pain
So who do i forgive?
the inner lost walks with me
I'm sorry

MEMORIES AND EGO

I can't remember when it happen
that moment
that moment
when i thought
he's the one
I can't remember

I can't remember the first time i said, I Love you
do you?

I can't remember you ever saying, I Love you back
do you?

I can't remember why you setup resident in my memories
do you?

I do remember your over the top Ego,
I do remember you are corny
I do remember asking myself why him!!?

I do remember
asking you for your jacket, when we first met because i was cold
You gave it to me with a big smile
You touched my hand
My heart was smitten

Now i remember what you said.
Forever or a day
I do remember
Can't you?

TOO OLD FOR FUN

her memory bank holds joyless memories
too grow old for fun
too old to remember how funny you are
too old to remember joy
too grow old for fun
too old to remember the sweet taste of kernel corn
remember
how to swing from a tree
remember
holding someone hand feels good
remember
laughing and dancing go together
too old to remember
sweet nectar of life
she has lived an unfinished life
too grow old to be unhappy

MY MOM SISTER BURNETTE

It's not the day, that you lose them
It's the days after
that hurts the most

My Mother's older sister passed away when i was a little girl
I remember three things about her
She had a nice smile, She had a funny laugh, and she loved music
Dinah Washington song " This Bitter Earth" was always playing on her
record player

Early one morning many years later, i walked into my Mother's bedroom
as she was staring out the window
I could see the tears on the side of her face
I asked her what was wrong?

My Mother replied, sometime i wake up reaching for the phone to call my
sister Burnette
I forget sometimes
Her sadness circle the room
she never turned around
She never said a another word
She kept staring out the window
Looking back into another time
It's not the day, that you lose them, that hurts the most
It's the
Days After
Days After
it's the
Days After
Days After

Sharon A. White

WHY ME, WHY ME, WHY ME

Lovers who Whisper
Lovers who Wait
Lovers who, can't love
Love me!!!!

GOD LETTER

Dear God

    My Mother Said when you talk to God you should tell him your whole name, you should tell him, what city you live in, you should tell him your address. She says this jokingly

    I believe you know, everything already, I believe you want us to talk to you when things are good. I believe you want us to talk to you when things are not that good. I believe the faith i have in you will help me make it everyday I breath.

    I need you Lord, I need your Grace, I need your Love, I need your Words of Wisdom, I need your Mercy asking for a Sister friend.

    But I'm one of those who will come when, I know I can't handle something without you. I can't do this alone Lord . . . I need you to hear my prayers, I need you to help my friends. They are in need of your Grace. your Love, your Word of Wisdom, your Mercy.

I have Faith in God
Knowing life's challenges are all around us
But I have you
I have Faith
I have Faith in knowing God walks with me
I have Faith in knowing my friends are in your hands
I have Faith

I have God

"For You., V.P.W., L,P.J.

P.S. Hi Jesus

It Told Me So

She never but a voice to her pain
She told it to be quiet
That's why her spirit can't love
It told me so
She likes her broken pieces
It told me that too

Broken Spirit
Broken Love
Broken Voice

How do I love thee?
How do I love thee?

she want to sing to her pain
she wants her voice not to hurt
she want her spirit to love

it told me so

How do I Love thee?
How do I Love thee?

she said
she doesn't want to be quiet anymore
she told me that too

I FELT

I felt love once
I felt adored twice
I felt cheap three times
i felt amuse most of the time
i felt burned once
I felt outside the box most of the time
I felt
I felt
Will i ever feel it again?

COLOR ME LOVE

He never liked my Blue Hair
I never liked his big Ears

He made me think out loud
I made him look good

He said he never wanted to love me
I Made him love me more

He never thought he would be with a Black Woman
He never thought he could love this woman, more
He never thought his family would walk away, from him

He never thought

He never thought her family would be part of the package deal
I call it family Love
He never thought he would be eating Sweet Potato Pie, at
Thanksgiving and not Pumpkin Pie
He never thought about Love over Color or Color over Love
He never thought he could Love a Woman like this

He never thought

He never thought he would marry a Black Woman
He never thought he would be this Happy

He just never thought about
what color is Love??
He never thought

WRONG LOVE

After i said i loved you
i felt a breeze kiss my cheek
flashes of light hide behind my eyes
what do you see?

After your eyes looked away
my heart singe itself
now what

After you walked away
i walk into the hurt
that kiss on my cheek stung like a bee

After i said i Loved you
You said
the Moon is a Planet
you never said
i love you

GRANNY LOVE

she like me
she like me
she loves me too

she likes holding my hand, when we stand next to each other
she likes making funny face at me
she gives me silly smile
she likes my spaghetti
i like who I'am when she's around
she comes over to give me Granny Love
it makes my heart laugh
she likes my oatmeal
i use cinnamon and nutmeg, it makes her happy
she hold my hand
she likes holding my hand
or is it me
she love me
i like who I 'am when she's around
she says, 'hey Granny are you getting crabby"
let me give you some Granny Love
I like making funny faces at her
and then I said 'hold my hand please"

My Brother New classmate the White Girl

she has long white blond hair,
she wasn't very tall, about my height little over 5'8
she had small blues eyes, and she has a big head not circus performer,
but big, just
big.

her skin was white, white, and white
she had a nice smile
her name was Betty Jane

We were standing next to each other, in the doorway of our house
she smelled like flowers
later that day she would said i smelled like ivory soap, I thought that
was funny
she was my brother new classmate
later that day we became new friends

she was smiling at me, before i could say anything
my brother said, meet my new girlfriend
i was thinking something, and then i went blank

i was laughing a little
i was giving them both a silly smile
he had talked to me about, this girl
we had long, long, talks about him and Betty Jane
his new classmate
his new classmate the girl
his new classmate the white girl

I kept thinking, fun times with Mom and Dad
she was my younger brother new girlfriend

what was i thinking, i asked myself
what was i really thinking?
i was thinking what would Maya Angelou say.
I was thinking what would Nikki Giovanni say.
I was thinking what would Sonia Sanchez say.
I was really thinking what would Martin L. King Jr, say.

before i could respond to what was happening in front of me, my
dear brother said talk to Mom and Dad for me, and for the second
time today, I went blank. And laughter was my response along with
just a little fear. On how my parents would!!!! react, not what they
would say about their baby boy dating his new classmate, the white
girl.

Times were changing, fun times in the White House

My brother said it again will you talk to Mom and Dad for me, you
know what to say, you and Dad talk about things like this all time,
how things are changing. You need to talk to Dad first, read him
some Nikki Giovanni, then tell him about Toni Morrison. I really like
this girl,' he said. I said do you really like this girl because she's white
or just teenage boy lust? He gave me that look, and he said I think
both more lust than anything else.

Several days later it was this big meeting, I like to call it Pow, Wow
going on in our living room. My parents had invited Betty Jane
parents over to talk. I walked into the living and everyone had this
silly, surprise look on their faces. My Mother was sitting at one end
of the sofa, my Dad was standing next to her and my brother John
Thomas was sitting in Dad's chair. Betty Jane parents, Levi and
Anna Rae Spence were sitting at the other end of the soft. There was
coffee and cookies on a small table, everyone had this puzzle look on
they face. I was standing there thinking, this could be a movie any
moment. Alfred Hitchcock would walk out and say cut, print. So
i said hello to her parents and My Mother said you kids should go

downstairs in the basement and let us talk, "as we were walking down stairs my, brother said to my back you have to to talk to them for us!!"

I responded who me? you can talk for yourselves i said, I also think we should listen to what they are saying. So all three of us were standing in the hallway of the basement listening. My Mom said she was scared for John Thomas coming over to see Betty Jane, and my Dad asked how do you guy really feel about this?

Betty Jane Mom said she thought John Thomas was a nice boy, but this is all new to our family. Kids today just don't understand what all this means. My Mom said she totally agreed. Mrs Anna Rae Spencer kept taking, she said, "I tried talking to Betty Jane about what could happen with her dating a Negro. That's when silence hit the room, i could hear my Mother counting to ten. My Mother looked at her hands she moved her legs around, Dad made a small sound, he knew his wife.

Then Mom said, "I'm not happy with my son dating your daughter." I looked at my brother tapped him on the back and whispered in his ear say good-bye to Betty Jane little brother , Mom is going in . . . . and then she said 'We all know how you people are, silence, silence, silence!!!

My brother looked at me and said Sabrina now you have to say something.

I'm not sure, what to say I told him, I walked into the living room everyone turned to looked at me, the words just start coming out. I have something to say, I think you are thinking of the past and yourself, we are different from you guys, we are not holding on to the past. We are not going to live our life in fear. I should be able to go to any school I want, I should be able to like who I want, when I want. You Parents can't stop how we fell about each other, just let it be. You are the ones making this a big deal. Everyone was looking at me with that puzzles look again.

My Dad was smiling and said, i think she's right my brother and Betty Jane were standing next to me and everyone said OK.

Betty Jane and her parents said good-bye, before they walked out the door Mr. Levi Spencer said John Thomas was welcome to come over any time. My Dad shook his hand, they had this nod between them. My Mom was looking at me, with this funny look on her face and then she said, you are something special. My Dad give me a nod and said 'I totally agree.' He whispered in my ear, OK Angela Davis.

At the end of the night my brother came to my room, he sat down on my bed, looked at me with joy and said thank you, thank you, thank you, Sabrina, you are the best.

I replied i want you to remember this moment, so when i come home with my French Man and i will. You will have to go toe to toe with Mom and Dad for me, silence. He walked out my room shaking his head, and laughing saying my sister, my sister, my sister.

GOD DAYS

tears covered my days
mists in the air
bluest skies
these are the days God talks to me

red eyes
dry skin
clear skies
these are the days God pushes me

i stand in stillness
i stand in pain
i stand covered in tears
i stand covered in hope

those are the days he carries me home

i stand with God

MY OTHER GIRL

her words are small
her steps are even smaller
she has big curious green eyes
when her brown Hair is cut short, she say look beautiful,
look beautiful
i don't always understand, the word coming out of her mouth
but i, listen, i listen
she say things like cake, cake
mom house
my mom says i should show her love
she has this silly laugh and it's really loud

I wonder
I wonder

can she understand love
i wonder does she know black from white
i wonder does she know, i melt with kindness for her
does she know
does she know

she gives me Frito's Chili Chips
to show me love
I wonder
does she love me back

Two-Five Ford Lane

Whenever I hear people say you can't go home again, I think maybe growing up on Two-Five Ford Lane was kinda of special. I always find, the need to come home

I have good memories about growing up on Ford Lane, it starts with me walking out the front door of our house and finding a large turtle in the front yard. This happens when you live with a small forest around you. Whenever they would build a new house they chopped down all those beautiful trees and you would see Jungle Book walking out the woods. I think that started my love for Mother Nature.

In the early years of living on Two-Five Ford Lane it was all about what tree you could climb fast and first. How far were you willing to run into the woods, and what new insect, bird, butterfly, grasshopper you saw first that day.

I saw beautiful blue birds, flying around. I was in awe looking at the red cardinals and robins sitting on every other tree branch. Pretty short furry tail rabbits looking at you wondering who are you, furry like squirrel's running the whole neighborhood, and lets not forget what scared me the most, long tail eyed field mouse.

As they say, that was back in the day, but I can say my parents house still has a small forest around it. And whenever I go home I sleep like a baby, the days seem to be longer, and sometime around midnight I hear the sounds of kids playing, laughing, in the middle of the street. I also hear music, lots of music playing everyone loves James Brown "Say it Loud I'm Black and I'm Proud," playing on the radio. This happen whenever I go home to Two-Ford Lane long lost memories, rush over me, some bad, but most are really good. I also feel the loss of family and friends.

Dad, Spring, Frank, Sue, Sharon, Robert, Billy, Nate, James, Corliss

I often find myself standing outside in the middle of the night in front of the house, I grew up in. Listening to the sound of the past, and thinking about how time has passed. You can still smell the woods. I like the smell of Two-Five Ford Lane, I like my memories. whoever said you can't go home again had it wrong. I think they never understand the real meaning of home. But I do home is always with you.

You just feel better when you do or is it just me.

My Grand Annie Bell

In the stillness of my days, I often find myself lost in thought of your words of wisdom, One of my favorite phase "If you Have Peace of Mind you Have Everything". Knowing one day I will see you again makes me smile. I sometime close my eyes and feel the warmth of you near me, My Grand Annie Bell Wright Ford

I remember once you told me you wasn't that fond of your name. I thought your name was beautiful, i thought you were beautiful. I have so many good memories of you it's like picking apple from a tree, one shiny memory after another.

On a clear day i can still see you sitting in the backyard of my Aunt Polly's house with her husband Spring Chicken. This was his favorite day he had more fun than anyone else on the 4th of July. Family and friends were all around when everything went wild and crazy, and you were right in the middle. Thinking of the memory makes me laugh, and smile.

When a spark from a firecracker propel into the air and guess what happen, two large boxes of Fireworks, blew up I mean. There was explosion, a Loud, Loud, Bang, Fireballs, and lets of Smoke more Firecrackers, the best lighting show you ever seen. It was Spectacular and everyone was running for cover but you. You just sat they watching, I never knew my mother could move so fast, but you sat on the lounge chair watching everyone run in circles. It was crazy fun, but you were laughing so hard that you started to hold your stomach and at some point everyone else stopped running and start laughing too.

It was the best 4ᵗʰ of July ever, we still laugh about it, Family Love.

Not everyone Will understand the love i have for my Grandmother Annie Bell and that's OK. If you never had a grandmother why would you. I do know this, you missed out completely. I had unconditional Love, everyday of her Life. I have two pictures of her hanging in my home, one in the kitchen, because she was a great cook, and the other picture is in my bedroom I talk to that one all the time.

I remember when people would say there are Angels among us Heaven must be missing an Angles because she is down here with us. I Knew that Angle, She was my Grandmother Annie Bell Wright Ford. I believe she had Invisible Wings, I believe I even saw them one day.

Colored Girl Can you Help Me

This was my first job in the Windy City, at the best Department store in Chicago, Marshall Fields. I felt like a small time girl going to the big city, even though I grew up only thirty miles away. I was overjoyed and ready to begin my new adventure.

I saw it coming

This silver haired petite white lady, wearing a high bun, shoulders back head high with wrinkles, on wrinkles, on wrinkles she had on one brown shoe and one black shoe walked right up to me with a smile and said, "Colored Girl Can You Help Me!" Those words just echoed out of her mouth.

I thought I saw the words flowing freely through the air and stop in the space between us. As I stood in silence I could hear this old Negro Spiritual song in my head "Swing Low Sweet Chariot Coming For To Carrying Me Home". And then she said it again, this time louder "Colored Girl Can You Help Me"

I think I was in shock, in shock, I had never been called that before. It's one thing to hear those words on TV, it's another to let the words circle around you and play tic-tac-toe with your emotions, I kept looking at her, thinking this is 1981. This petite white lady kept looking at me with wonder.

Still in silence I realize, I was angry how much of that old Spiritual song was ringing in my ear, "Swing Low Sweet Chariot"

I walked a little closer to her without even thinking. I said in a nice nasty tone "You Can't Call Me That Anymore"

She looks bewildered at what I said, I felt sorry for her, but I was still angry, this little voice in my head said remember what Mom said respect your elders. This petite white lady spoke in a clear soft voice, "That Is What I Always Called You People." I looked at her without feeling anything and pointed to my name tag, My name is Sharon if you want me to help you.

You May call me Miss. Sharon without hastening she said Miss Sharon will you help me? I asked why do you have on one brown shoe and one black shoe?

The Moral of this Story : Time and space have nothing to do with how someone chooses to see color or use the words and you are never too old to learn something new . . . And never, never ever, ever as long as there is night and day walk up to and me say

"Colored Girl Can You Help Me"

I RATHER

No matter how i feel
No matter how long i wait
No matter how many times i dream about you
I rather eat
Dirt
Then admit I love you

No matter how you love me
No matter how much i like your kisses
No matter how many times i dream about you
I rather eat
Uncooked Chitlin's
Then admit I love you

No matter how sad I'am
No matter how much I miss you
No matter how many times i dream about you
I rather
Jump out of a airplane without a parachute
Then admit I love you
I rather!!!!

Sharon A. White

LEADING MAN

He is a shadow of a man with popcorn eyes, and the voice of a
Shakespeare actor
Who whines his days away
This ghostly figure of a man has secrets
with has everlasting jest for life
he flow sweetly touched by his own ripeness
he is a leading man you know
he often weeps when he is alone
we only know him as the jester
this ghostly figure of a man sings to himself with pride and joy he
thinks he's Frank Sinatra, knowing only six words to the song
"It Was A Very Good Year," he sings over, over again
you know he is a leading man

Spirit Voice

Windy days have a beat to them
Windy days have rhythm
you have to be open to hear
the great spirit voice

i hear a song in the wind
it hum's within my soul
i hear a song in the wind

it takes me up, it takes me down
blow baby, blow baby
I feel the kiss of the wind rushing over me
it move me up, it take me down
sing my song

windy days make me think of making love
i hear a song in the wind
i feel the oneness of you
i hear the great spirit voice

ROOFTOP GARDEN

I'm lonely she says
what surprises her the most, she said it out loud
I'm lonely she says again
maybe this time the birds will notice
It's all about the space in between
I'm lonely she says louder as she looks out over, her rooftop garden
maybe this time daffodils will give her wink. I think Daisies were
weeping for me, I saw a tear running down a petal, notice me.

Afro swinging in the wind, red lips turned down, her skin has been
kissed by the sun. Her long slender body leans against the brick wall
waiting, waiting to me be notice, waiting to be forgiven, waiting to
say I'm sorry, I do apologize. No excuses, no blame, no tears, it was
my own laziness of love. Please forgive me for not loving you the right
way, please forgive me for not opening my heart to greet you each day
you loved me.

"I'm Lonely, I'm Lonely" she says out loud, but this time she repeats
the last words he said to her. "God is always the answer and the
answer is always Love"

DON'T YOU SEE ME CRYING HERE

she start crying when her mother walked out the door
she never cries
her whole face change to high drama
her performance started with tears, jumping up and down, and
talking loud
her performance was strong
my response was calm, I asked why are you crying like that?
she squeeze one eye shut, one tear came out
she squeeze the other eye shut, one more tear came out
she is good,
i was trying not to laugh
her shoulders moved up and down
she needed more drama, so she fail to the floor on her knees
she put her hands, over her face
only to peek through to see what i was doing
i laughed out loud
this was good drama
i was still laughing
she made a fist
i think that little fist hit the air
i was laughing, really laughing now
she has good drama
she made this crying sound and said
don't you see me crying here?
she cried out
she said it again, this time louder
don't you see me crying here?

I said
Hollywood should be knocking, any minute
knock, knock, knock
little girl grand performance
Smelly Cat, smelly cat what have you ate today

i was looking at this little girl with a new eye
she had everyone jumping to her tune
Little girl, silly smart
Hollywood, Hollywood
then she said it again
don't you see me crying here?
my only response
you look pretty when you cry,
go for it
silence!!!!!

IT STARTS FROM HOME

the first time it happen i felt numb
the second time it happen i was shocked
the third time it happen resentment sat in
I now have a real understanding what my grandmother
was saying
at first i thought she was being old fashioned
but my grandmother was right
racism starts at home

the first time i was called a nigger
a group of us were walking down the street in front of the men's dorm
the second time i was called a nigger
at a stoplight next to a school bus
the third time i was called a nigger
two young white men in a car
this time it came with spit
homeschool 101
racism so starts from home

Popsicle Orange Jumpsuit

a four year old little boy name JJ told me to smell the crack of his butt
i asked him, why would you say that
his response, you were mean to me today
i replied that's not a nice thing to say
under my breath i said Smelly Cat, Smelly Cat what have you ate today
i called on my friends Jesus and he said, Could you do the?
i said Smelly Cat, Smelly Cat how good would i look in a Popsicle orange jumpsuit Smelly Cat, Smelly Cat what have you ate today
Under my breath I said Smelly Cat, Smelly Cat, would my friends visit me in jail?

a four year old little boy name Chance and he was going to step on my hand and kick me hard
i asked him, why would you say that?
his response, you're not listening to me
i replied, that's not a nice thing to say
under my breath i said Smelly Cat, Smelly Cat, what have you ate today
i called on my friend Jesus, and he said "Can you do the time?"
Smelly Cat, Smelly Cat how good would i look in a Popsicle orange jumpsuit
under breath my i said Smelly Cat, Smelly Cat, would my friends visit me in jail?

I talk to my Mother today she said you should get out more, you will never find a man, staying home so much
i replied not all skinny girls, have a man they have problems too
I called on my friend Jesus and he said yes Jesus loves you, yes Jesus loves you
under my breath i said Smelly Cat, Smelly cat what have you ate today
Smelly Cat, Smelly Cat, how good would i look in a Popsicle orange

jumpsuit.
Smelly Cat, Smelly Cat would my friends visit me in jail?
Smelly Cat, response
Make new friends in Jail

CAN YOU, DO YOU

do you have any juice in your turnip's??
or has your sauce dried up
do your wheels still roll?
or do you use WD40
has the well run dry?
or are you still a fine wine
have you given up on salt?
or do you obay, the dry rub
do you still eat Pork?
do you still eat chicken?
or do you shake and bake
have you surrender to love?
or have you just lost the recipe

I Kissed a white Guy

he has sapphire blue eyes
that said twinkle, twinkle
he wear tight black jeans, with shiny black cowboy boots
his hair is black as midnight
i think he glows in the dark
snow white would call him her prince charming
i just call him white boy
he called me essence
he asked me, have you dated a white guy before?
i replied no, but I'm curious
he replied, let me be your first
i give him a mischievous smile
his blue eyes said
twinkle, twinkle
he asked me, may i kiss you
i replied not everyone knows how to kiss, i think it's a lost art
he give me a devilish smile
he replied, essence let me, be the first white guy to show you his art.
i laughed, i was amused by his words
he said you scared
i replied who me
again his blue eyes
said twinkle, twinkle
but this time, i felt him pulling me in
he said i like you
i said, i can't take you home
he said again i like you
i said my family would never understand
he replied i like you first, your family come later
kiss me
he whispered softly in my ear, let it happen
those damn, blue eyes
yes i whispered

his lips were sweet, his touch was strong, he pulled me in i thought
he would never let me go,
i was breathing hard
i smell lavender
i kept thinking, danger Will Robinson, danger Will Robinson
we both take a step back
silence, then more silence
devilish smiles ran across both our face
i said, may i kiss you
he replied, yes essence
twinkle, twinkle, twinkle

SHE THOUGHT, I THOUGHT

She thought i was too young to understand
What a black eye was
She thought i wasn't listening to
Her cries for help
She thought loving him more would work
She thought wrong
I thought she should leave
She told me one day when you grow up you will understand
I thought she was Dumb
I
grew up and I still don't understand

ABSOLUTE SHOW

I happen to be a disbeliever in the
Political System of Man
I call it Political System of Egoism
I call it Political System of Flaws
I call it Political System of Loyalists
I call it Political System of Bias
I call it Political System of Greed
I call it Political System of the Absolute Show
it's too complicate for me to believe in
The Political System of Man

But I was Praying for him!!!!!!
But I can believe in
The Political System of Hope

I MISS

I miss Love
I miss the soft caress of love
I miss the scent of love
I miss the rustling sound of love
Can you sing, me a love song?

I miss love spooning
I miss your warm breath on my neck, it makes me wiggle
can you sing, me a love song?

I miss being amorous
I miss the air between us
you smell like oldspice
Can you sing me, a love sing?

I miss love
do love miss me?
i wonder

HE BELONG TO ANOTHER

i lost my beloved in the morning mists he belong to another
Tear drops taste of honey wine, sweet surrender into darkness
Sorrow escape my lips night and day
Forever will i moan
Forever will your fever haunt me
Forever will i miss the best of your heart
i lost my beloved to another
i lay in silence waiting your return
now naked with fear
all hope is gone
free me from my sorrow
love me again

I HATE SNOW

I hate the beauty of the snow
I'm as lonely as a snowflake
one single flake at a time
take the whiteness away
break all the ice crystal
i hate the beauty of the snow

i know snow is really lonely
kinda like me
one single cell
one single vapor
one single me

PAPER UMBRELLA

Soon or Later I'm going to open the door to love
Should it be on Wednesday, when paper umbrella
Come back in season or should i surprise myself and
wait till Sunday when God ears are open to the weak
to the hopeless and to those who just want a love of their
own
Sunday sounds good to me

WILD WINDS

I Dream of running wild with the wind
Bare chest and free
Feather I'm not
Beautiful I'm
Rumbling winds carry me across the clear Sky
I dreamt i ran with the Bulls
Amazing
I know where I'm going
Take me home and marry me
With Joy

PASSION FLEES

Passion flees my darling
Bitter heart runs wild with desire
Never will i let you kill my spirit
Never will i love thee again
Never will i live without passion
My grief, My grief, My darling
Rediscovering what made love
Beautiful again

RUMBLING SPIRIT

To open old emotions
To close old fears
To call on God for something more than me
To smell a new day
I pray day and night to prolong
My rumbling spirit of doubt
To call on God
To ask for forgiveness
To say thank you
To breath again with a new spirit
To ask God
Can i do all things??

WHY, WHY, WHY

Why Love?   They call me Miss. Independent
Why Hate?   You have to give up yourself for hate
Why Submission?   Would you leave yourself for love
What would you say for love?   Good Morning Honey

MY BROTHERS

they used to put frogs in my bed
spider in my shoes
lady bugs on my pillow
I love them all
they showed me how to ride a bike, fix a bike, climb trees, fight boys,
cut grass, play baseball, make pancakes, play card, like sports
I love them all
one said don't do drugs
one showed me what drugs not to do
one showed me how to drive a car
one showed me how to fix a washing machine
one said don't be a sissy
I said I'm a girl
one showed me how to wrestles
they all showed me how to run fast
one said you don't have sex, with everyone just because they ask
one said be a lady
they all kept the wolves away
one said it would be nice to have a husband, boyfriend, or whoever
make you happy, but you should always know how to take care of yourself.
all of them agreed on one thing
I should learn how to
Cook!!
really
and i still love them all
My Brothers, My Brothers, My Brothers, My Brothers

"PANDORA KNOCKED ON THE WRONG DOOR TODAY"

Pandora knocked on my door today
I opened the door with a big smile

I invited her in for tea
In the back of my mind i was thinking
She looks impressive

I asked Pandora
What can I do for you today?
She responded with a enormous smile
Her eyes shine like gold
Her skin was smooth as silk
Her lips were glowing
You could see in her eye's, Pandora came to play
Under my breath i said
"Your Lips are Stunning"

She spoke in a soft whisper
I know this trick, it works on men
it has a undue power, but it works
Why would she think it would work on me?
This was a game
and that was the game changer

You are not paying attention, she said
I was thinking about your lips, I said
Your lipstick has my attention
That lipstick is sexy
I responded with a smile
Go on Pandora, I said

She smiled back and whispered softly
I go door to door selling my specialties
Do you want to know the special of today?
my response was yes
With that enormous smile she said
"Envy"
and then she, said it again

"Envy" you know the word
this time her eyes were laughing
Her face was glowing
Her eyes
Even though she was still smiling
i could see a change in the way she was looking at me
Her new smile made my body shake
Pandora wasn't playing anymore
Under my breath I said a Fools game
She thinks I'm a
Fool.

Pandora looked like she was walking to the mirror, but she really was flowing, her hands were moving and her hair was flowing with each movement. She was enjoying herself, she was laughing at the look on my face. This is when she pulled out a purple and gold lipstick tube, she pushed a small bottom and this is when I understood "Envy" Pink Passion was the name of the lipstick that made me feel sexy and beautiful. I haven't been able to find it in years.

Pandora had the look of pure satisfaction on her face, that made me laugh out loud, in true form she asked. Are you laughing at me? I nod yes and kept laughing at her with satisfaction on my face too. We stand they looking at each other, a few minutes. Pandora said this is why I like to go door to door to see the look on people faces. When they realize Greed, Overindulgence, Bigotry, are all part of who you are, just waiting to see it come out. I'm just the one person to help you see it.

That little speech of hers made me pause,

I kept looking at her with wonderment, and she still had this silly smile on her face. I said Pandora you have no ideal who I'm and what i believe, now she was really laughing at what i was saying. the next thing I said made her silent, I'm a child of GOD. I start my day with a "Thank You" do you want to know why? I know where my power comes from, there is nothing more important to me than my faith. There are three key things you should know, GOD has given me the power, "To Love Myself," to forgive and you will be forgiven and to pray.

So Pandora are you selling Bibles today.

"PRETTY FROM THE BACK"

How often do you look in the mirror, and tell your reflection not today, and the next thing you hear your reflection saying back to you. OK, OK,!!!!!
But can I wish you Happy Birthday . . .

This was how my Thirty-Second Birthday began me having a mind altering moment
Happy Birthday to me, Happy Birthday to me . . .

It's early Sunday morning I realize I left my bedroom window open, when this cool breeze blows through and kissed my skin. I smell my garden, my room smells like lavender and rosemary. This is the best time to dream, sunlight has cast a golden glow around me, it feels good I just want to lay here and dream about him. Or should I go back to the mirror and have another mind altering moment, I think not.! I can't sleep, I can't close my eyes I have this image of my brother looking at me with sadness and pity.

I need more time to dream
No more time to dream

I kept thinking about what I saw in my brother eyes, compassion because he love me, but pity was what I saw first he was looking directly at me, his eyes said everything. Even I could see that through his thick glasses, I could still see the pity, felt it to.

My big brother surprised me last night he, unexpectedly gave me a airline ticket to Hawaii and told me it was time. He began to tell me how he passes my room, year after year and if you're not working, you are in your room reading a book or working in your garden. And in the middle of the night you are looking out your window waiting for him to come back. He then said you need to make a change, that's why I giving you a airline ticket to Hawaii for your birthday.

Remember what Mom used to say Prince Charming Can't Find you Hiding in your Bedroom remember, she also said you're such a pretty girl it's not too late. But her most famous saying was "You Look Better from From The Back" Mom has some good one liners. It's time sis, in fact I can't take it another day without telling you how I really feel. I would like to think I was still dreaming, but this was real. I never thought my brother could talk soon much, I never knew he felt this way and he wasn't finished yet.

It was me born with a disability, not you. I remember when you had a light in your eye. I'm the one you should listen to, it's time Sis. You need to be honest with yourself, you can't hide behind hurt any more, you can't hide behind the loss any more. You can't hide behind me!!! I have a life. I have my art, I have my music. I have women on call. He said this with a smile on his face. What he said made me laugh and cry at the same time, we both were laughing out loud at what he said. It felt good to laugh with him.

He gave me a big hug and walked me to the door, it's time he said. I have a car waiting for you. Your plane departs in three hours your luggage is already in the car, don't look back Sis was his last words before he kissed me good-bye
As I was walking out the door i began to think of one of Mom one liners, but then I stopped myself and decide to have my own "How I Got My Groove Back, "Life has to be Lived" and the best one "Pretty From the Back"

The Beginning . . .

ABOUT THE AUTHOR

I grew up in Gary, Indiana with my parents, Richard, Irma Jean White, four Brothers, one Sis, a dog name Duke and a Cat name Pretty. When my grandfather passed away my father brought home his library of books including lets of Bibles and other Religions books. My favorite was "The Power Of Positive Thinking" by Norman Vincent Peale, even as teenager I knew this book was important. I still read my grandfather old book. The books I was into reading were by authors Richard Wright, Langston Hughes, Gwendolyn Books, James Baldwin and the Black Panther newspaper I was trying to understand the why, of racialism.

My Mother wouldn't buy me a Barbie, when I was a little. Many years later she told me why, "That was not the image I wanted for my little Girl," you needed to love your blackness first and not let the outside world make you think less of your Beauty.

Sharon White currently lives in Madison, Wis.
This is her first book of Poetry, Short Stories.

In memory of my Father.
I will miss you forever.